American Horse Tales

Nowheresville

by Catherine Hapka

Penguin Workshop

For Lance, a good little horse—CH

PENGUIN WORKSHOP
An imprint of Penguin Random House LLC, New York

First published in the United States of America by Penguin Workshop,
an imprint of Penguin Random House LLC, New York, 2022

Visit us online at penguinrandomhouse.com.

Library of Congress Cataloging-in-Publication Data is available.

Printed in the United States of America

ISBN 9780593225295   10 9 8 7 6 5 4 3 2 1 COMR

Chapter 1
Goodbye, Philly

"Nat! Natalie Anne Morris, where are you?"

I looked up and blinked. Where was I? Lost, as usual, in my favorite graphic novel, *The Boy Next Door*. I'd read it about a million times, and I'd just reached the part where the hero, Boy, rescues a famous movie star from a volcano. The drawings were so amazing, I could practically smell the lava!

But as I blinked again, I realized I wasn't standing at the edge of a volcano. I was lying on the bare wooden floor in my bedroom. Instead of lava, I smelled grease from the pizza place across the street.

That smell was familiar. But my room didn't look familiar anymore. My bed; the battered, old overstuffed bookcase; and the vintage steamer trunk where I kept my art supplies was gone. So was the drafting table Mom had helped me build out of scrap lumber we found on the curb in front of the Korean market.

The room should have looked bigger when empty, but it seemed even tinier than before. My friend Johari always joked that my room was the size of her closet, but I didn't mind. It was cozy. And all mine.

Well, actually, not anymore . . .

I sighed and slowly stood up. The only thing left in the room was my army-surplus backpack with its cool, nerdy pins and a ratty Philadelphia Eagles bumper sticker covering a rip in the side. I shoved *The Boy Next Door* into the bag, then glanced around one last time.

"Bye, room," I said.

My voice echoed off the empty floor and walls.

"Nat!" My mom's voice drifted up again from the street three stories below the apartment. "Get down here!"

I stuck my head out the window. A crowd was gathered on and around the stoop, spilling onto the street and blocking traffic. "Coming!" I hollered back.

Soon I was down there, being swarmed by a bunch of neighbors cooing about how much they'd miss me and Mom. Ms. Battaglia shoved a paper bag of homemade cookies into my hand, while Mr. Kim tucked a few dollars into my backpack before I could stop him.

"We'll miss you, kotyonok," Mrs. Orlov said, enveloping me in a garlic-and-dill-scented hug that made me flash back to all the times I'd hung out in her apartment, watching her cook when Mom had late classes at the university.

"Me too," I said. "I can't believe we're really doing this."

I glanced at our car, double-parked nearby with a rented trailer hooked to the back. Inside were all of our worldly possessions, minus some furniture we'd donated to the rescue mission. My mother was busy trying to shove in one more box.

Then my best friends, Johari and Blue, pushed past the grown-ups. Blue grabbed me and kissed me on both cheeks—that was her thing lately, ever since she saw someone do it in an old movie—and Johari punched me on the arm so hard it hurt.

"I can't believe you're moving to the middle of

Nowheresville." Johari sounded angry, but I knew it wasn't aimed at me.

"You and me both," I told her. "I mean, how is Hazem's even going to stay in business without me?" It was supposed to be a joke, but thinking about my favorite falafel place made me sad (and a little hungry).

Blue nodded, which made her long, blond bangs flop into her face. "They probably don't even have falafel way out there," she said. "We'll have to FedEx it to you or something."

"Forget falafel." Johari tugged at a stray curl of her Afro. "How are you going to keep drawing the adventures?"

"Good question," I muttered. I was currently working on a series of urban-fantasy comics I called *The Adventures of Urbanna Urban*. In each story, the hero had to battle shape-shifters, vampires, and other supernatural creatures in her Philadelphia neighborhood, which looked a lot like mine. Okay, there were no ghouls or goblins threatening mayhem on my block. But the rest was the same— row houses and apartment buildings, the pizza place, a laundromat, Ms. Battaglia's law office, and various other businesses all jumbled together. Colorful graffiti decorated brick and stone walls; funky music and smells drifted through the air; and people of all shapes, sizes, and colors were everywhere, all the time, ready to become the next hero, villain, or victim in Urbanna's adventures. Where was I supposed to find inspiration now? Staring at a bunch of trees and birds?

Thinking about that—about not being *here* anymore, where I belonged—made me feel shaky, uncertain, and sad, which was pretty much the opposite of my usual self. I wasn't even sure who I was supposed to *be* now. I was used to thinking of myself in a few specific ways: A city girl. An artist. A nerd. Definitely indoorsy.

Those things worked for me in Philadelphia. But now I was supposed to live way out in rural Pennsylvania, hours from everyone and everything I'd ever known in the entire ten-and-almost-three-quarters years of my life.

"I wish your mom got a job here in Philly," Blue said.

"Or if you had to be in the boonies, she could've stuck to, like, the Main Line or Jersey," Johari added. "At least then you could take the train in sometimes, like Anika does since she moved out to Haverford."

I nodded and glanced at Mom again. Even though I was furious with her for making us move, I was proud of her, too. She'd raised me on her own ever since my dad died when I was a baby. For almost

7

as long as I could remember, she'd held down a full-time office job at Drexel University while also taking classes there to become a PA—that's short for physician assistant. A PA can do just about anything a doctor can do, and I knew Mom was going to be great at her new job.

The only problem? That new job was working for a doctor way out in central Pennsylvania, an over-two-hour drive from Philly. Like Johari had said: Nowheresville.

"I bet she could've found a job in the city if she'd kept looking," Blue said.

"Yeah," Johari agreed. "There are way more people who need medical care here than in some tiny hick town."

"I know." I watched out of the corner of my eye as Mom hugged our landlord, Mr. Moore. "I told her she shouldn't take the first thing that came along.

It's not like they were going to boot her from her old job. But she said I didn't understand."

If you asked me, *Mom* was the one who didn't understand. How could she? She'd lived in a bunch of different places before settling in Philly to marry my dad. But this was the only home I'd ever known.

Mr. Moore rushed over, his wild, curly, gray-and-black hair sticking out in all directions as usual. "Natalie, darling girl," he exclaimed. "You have to convince your mother to abandon this foolish plan and stay here where she belongs!" He threw both hands in the air. "The place is going to fall apart without you two!"

He probably wasn't even kidding. Mom was super handy—she could fix or build just about anything. She'd taught me plumbing, carpentry, and everything else she knew from the time I was probably too young to be messing with that kind of stuff. But every time I banged my thumb with a hammer or scratched myself on a rusty pipe, she said it was important to be able to take care of yourself. So I kept trying, and now I was almost as good as she was. The two of us had fixed just about everything in our building over the years, in exchange for a discount on rent. Mr. Moore would *definitely* miss us.

"Never mind, John," Mom told him with a laugh. "You'll have to figure out how to swing a hammer yourself, that's all." She checked her watch. "We'd better get this show on the road, Nat. We've got a long drive."

"Oh my gosh, I can't believe this is happening," Blue wailed, wrapping her arms around me like a spider monkey. Johari grabbed us both, squeezing so hard I could barely breathe.

"I'll miss you guys like crazy." Suddenly, I was

crying. We all were. "Promise to text me every hour on the hour, okay?"

"Definitely," Johari said fiercely, while Blue just sobbed.

The next few minutes felt like one of those breaks between panels in a graphic novel, where one minute something is happening, and then suddenly it's the next day. Before I knew it, I was in the car waving to everyone I'd ever known as they got smaller and smaller behind us. Then we turned at the end of the block, and they were gone.

I stared out the window, trying to memorize every inch of the familiar skyline for as long as I could still see it.

Chapter 2
Hello, Nowheresville

"We've made it!" Mom sang out. "Welcome to Daisy Dell—there's the sign, see?"

I looked up from my sketch pad. I'd been doodling for the past hour or so, ever since we'd left the last remnants of civilization behind for a nonstop panorama of green fields, trees, and the occasional housing development or herd of cows. Yes, literal cows.

"Where's the town?" I asked.

Mom rolled her eyes. "Don't play dumb, Natalie. You know our new home isn't going to be exactly like the city."

Daisy Dell didn't look much like the small towns I'd seen in movies. It was just a handful of old houses, a tiny brick post office, a church, a hair salon, a gas station, and a pizza place. Before I knew it, we were passing the COME BACK SOON! sign.

"Wait, that's it?" I said. "Where's the hospital where you'll be working? And did I miss the one-room schoolhouse where I'll be doing my readin' and writin' and 'rithmetic?"

Mom shot me a sour look. Driving isn't her favorite activity, and she'd been doing it for a looooong time by then, so I knew I was pushing it.

"Very funny," she said in a tone that conveyed she didn't think it was funny at all. "We'll pass my new office in a minute. And your school is a few miles from here—you'll take the bus to get there."

I brightened slightly. "There's a bus?"

"A school bus," Mom said. "Not like SEPTA buses. Come on, Nat, I know you've seen this stuff on TV, at least."

I shrugged. "So you're saying I'm stuck at home when you can't drive me places."

"I'll get you a bicycle." She sounded distracted. She was peering ahead as we neared a couple of modern-looking buildings with a parking lot out front. "Look, there it is—the medical center." Now she sounded excited. "I'll slow down so you can check it out. Dr. Hernandez—on the sign there, above the dental office, see? She's my new boss."

"Okay," I said, trying to sound interested for her sake. "That's cool."

She shot me a small smile. "I hope you'll give this a chance, Nat. You've always been so adventurous. I never thought you'd . . . Anyway, it reminds me of where I grew up."

Mom had lived on a farm in Virginia until she was around my age, feeding chickens, riding bareback and barefoot on her neighbors' ornery pony, and picking apples right off the trees. Her stories had seemed charming and fun back in Philly.

But that was then, and this was now. Daisy Dell was as different from Philadelphia as it could be. For instance, I spotted yet another small herd of cows grazing within view of Mom's job.

"Cows," I murmured, wondering if I could turn them into some kind of foe for Urbanna. Zombie cows? Fairy cows?

"The cows are cute, aren't they?" Mom looked over again. "Hey, maybe once we're settled in, we can talk about getting a pet."

I blinked at her, still half lost in my thoughts.

"Like a cow?"

"Not a cow, silly." She chuckled. "But a cat or dog isn't out of the question. You've always wanted a pet, and they're allowed in our new rental."

Mr. Moore was allergic to everything and didn't allow animals in his building. So although I'd had to leave my friends and everything else I'd ever known or cared about behind, maybe I could finally get a dog. I supposed that counted as a silver lining, even if it was only a sliver of silver.

⁓

"Here we are!" Mom announced ten minutes later. "Home sweet brand-new home."

I didn't dare look up from my phone. Blue had just texted me a selfie of her and Johari looking sad as they ate chicken shawarma at Hazem's.

Don't rub it in!!! I texted back quickly, then finally looked up.

I wasn't sure "brand-new" was how I'd describe what I saw. But it was big. Mom had told me we'd be renting a house, not an apartment, though that hadn't really sunk in until now.

"This is all for us?" I said, squinting up at the second-story windows.

The house had pale-blue siding, a front porch, a carport, and a tiny patch of grass. On one side was a cornfield, and on the other were more houses.

I crawled out of the car, my legs rubbery after the long ride. The porch steps creaked when I climbed them. "This place isn't going to collapse on us, is it?" I asked.

"Stop it, Nat. Come on in and take a look."

I followed Mom into a small foyer with a wooden staircase and a carpeted floor. There was a living room off to one side and a kitchen at the back.

"Go upstairs and check out your room," Mom

urged, dropping her purse on a table in the foyer. She'd explained that this place came partially furnished, which was why we'd given away some of our stuff. "It's the door on the left at the top of the stairs. Your bathroom's right next to it."

I was three or four steps up when her words seeped into my brain. I stopped short. "*My* bathroom?"

Mom grinned. "Two and a half baths, baby. No more arguing over who gets to shower first."

Another silver lining. My own bathroom! Even Johari had to share with her sister.

I peeked into my bathroom (MY bathroom!), which had yellow tiles and a full-size tub. Then I stepped into my new bedroom.

"Wow," I blurted out. It was enormous—easily four times larger than my old room.

I dropped my backpack onto the mattress and

wandered around, a little confused by all that space. One window showed the tiny backyard, which was just a concrete slab surrounded by a tall wooden fence. The other looked over the place next door.

Now that I was paying attention, I realized the building right next door wasn't actually a house. It was a cute red barn with a fenced paddock out front and a larger field in back that extended behind my new house. I wondered if it was where the local cows stayed at night.

Then a boy emerged from the house on the far side of the barn. He looked about twelve years old, though it was hard to tell since he was staring down at his phone as he walked. He slid open the barn door and disappeared inside.

Moments later he reappeared, this time leading a horse. Yes, an honest-to-goodness horse! For some reason, I hadn't been expecting that—the only horses I'd seen in real life were police horses and a few in parades. This one was pure white with big, dark eyes.

That was all I noticed about the horse, because now I also had a better view of the kid leading it. My eyes widened.

"Whoa," I whispered. "It's Boy!"

I could hardly believe it. The boy next door looked almost exactly like the hero of *The Boy Next Door*!

"Oh my gosh, oh my gosh!" My heart pounded as I wondered whether to text my friends, grab my copy of the graphic novel to double-check what I was seeing, or just faint on the spot. Instead, I ran out of the room at top speed. I had to meet this guy!

I clattered down the stairs. Mom was carrying in a box from outside. "There you are," she said. "The trailer's open if you want to grab your—"

"Be right back," I cut her off, sprinting out through the open front door.

Boy and horse were in the paddock when I got there. They both looked over as I skidded to a stop by the fence.

"Oh, hi," the boy said. "You must be the new renters."

"I'm Nat," I blurted out. "Natalie Morris. We just moved in."

His smile was friendly. "I'm Logan Reed." He waved toward the other house. "My parents and I live over there. And this is Ghost."

"Huh?" I flashed back to the story where Boy battles a gang of spectral villains. "A ghost?"

Logan laughed and patted the horse. "This guy right here—he's one of my horses, and his name is Ghost. He's my latest project. I'm retraining him."

"Oh okay." I grinned back at him. It was weird

looking straight at the real-life version of my hero. My breathing was shallow, and I wasn't sure what to do with my hands. Was this what having a crush was like?

I wasn't totally sure, since I'd never had one before. But I'd heard Johari's older sister and her friends talk about boys enough to have a pretty good idea. So now what was I supposed to do?

Play it cool, Nat, I told myself. *You're cool as a frozen cucumber.*

I carefully stretched one hand over the fence toward the horse. "He's pretty," I said. "Um, can I pet him?"

"Sure. Oh hey, I think he likes you!"

The horse had just turned his head to snuffle at my hand. His nose felt soft, like the velvet collar on Mom's favorite vintage coat, and his eyes were fringed with long lashes. I also couldn't help noticing a smell that reminded me of the Philadelphia Zoo.

"Wow, he usually doesn't pay much attention to people he doesn't know." Logan sounded surprised and pleased. "Do you ride?"

"No way," I said quickly. "I prefer to keep my feet on the ground, thank you very much."

Ghost nudged at my hand and let out a funny little noise, like an engine starting up in the distance: *chuff-chuff-chuff*.

"He's cute, though," I said, giving the horse one more rub on the nose before shooting Logan a sidelong look. "By the way, did anyone ever tell you that you look *exactly* like—"

"Natalie!" Mom's shout interrupted.

Looking annoyed, she came marching toward us. After trading quick introductions with Logan, who promised to let his parents know we were here, she dragged me home to unpack.

Chapter 3
The Boy (and Horse) Next Door

When I woke up the next morning, I didn't know where I was for a second. Then I remembered: my new bedroom in Nowheresville.

I sat up and stretched, wondering what was for breakfast. Normally on Sundays, Mom and I walked three blocks to our favorite diner. Obviously that wasn't going to be happening here.

As I sat in bed feeling hungry and a little cranky, a faint thump-thump-thumping sound drifted in through the half-open window. I got up and looked out just in time to see a brown horse leap over a stack of straw bales in the front paddock. I guessed that was Logan in the saddle, though I couldn't see his face with his helmet on.

The horse galloped on toward a pair of big, blue barrels lying on their side. I held my breath until it landed on the far side of the obstacle.

"That must be one of his other horses," I whispered, remembering that Logan had mentioned having more than one. This horse looked a lot livelier than Ghost. When Logan brought it to a stop, it pranced and tossed its head.

I opened the window wider so I could lean out. "Nice jumping!" I shouted, waving.

Logan squinted up at me, grinned, and waved back. "Thanks!" he called.

I realized I was still in my pajamas—oops,

embarrassing! But whatever. Johari's sister always said boys knew nothing about fashion.

Still, I resisted grabbing the first clothes I found (yesterday's shorts and my favorite Phillie Phanatic T-shirt) and instead dug through half-unpacked boxes until I found a cute skort and the adorable short-sleeved pink bomber jacket my friends and I had found at a vintage shop on South Street. Why not look my best for the Boy Next Door?

As I headed downstairs, I checked my phone for new texts, but there was nothing. That wasn't surprising—on Sundays Johari's family went to church, and Blue always slept late. I was sure they'd check in soon.

Mom was in the kitchen making scrambled eggs. She'd insisted on unpacking the kitchen stuff first, so it looked fairly normal in there, unlike the explosion of large cardboard boxes that were scattered throughout the rest of the house.

"Morning, Nat," she said with a yawn. "Ready to get to work?"

Work? Oh right. Mom had said something last night about wanting to replace the leaky sink trap in her bathroom and maybe paint a couple of rooms before she started her new job the next day.

"Actually, I was thinking about going over to say hi to Logan." I flopped into a chair. "He's out there right now."

"You can do that after." Mom slid a plate of eggs and toast in front of me. "Eat up."

An hour later, we were in her bathroom with tools spread everywhere. I'd hung my bomber jacket on the door handle, not wanting to mess it up.

"By the way," Mom said, her voice slightly muffled by the fact that her head was inside the sink cabinet. "Don't forget day camp starts tomorrow."

"Day camp?" I looked up from searching the tool bag for the right-size pliers. "What are you talking about?"

She pulled out her head. "Day camp," she said again, like that cleared anything up. "I'm sure I mentioned it. You obviously can't sit around the house all summer by yourself while I'm at work. Plus, it'll give you a chance to meet some local kids before school starts."

Meeting kids sounded like a good idea. Back in Philly, I spent summers hanging out at Blue's house—her mom and her mom's girlfriend both worked from home—or at Johari's when her sister was around to watch us. Even when everyone else was busy, I could chill with Mrs. Orlov or Mr. Moore. Sometimes, I could even convince Mr. Moore to take me to the comic-book shop to check if new issues of *The Boy Next Door* had come in, since he collected old-school Superman comics himself.

There were no comic-book shops in Daisy Dell. And no friends to stay with, either. Still, who needed day camp? I was almost eleven, which seemed plenty old enough to stay home on my own.

"Are you sure?" I said. "Day camp sounds expensive, and you said money was tight with the move and all . . ."

"Don't worry about that, Nat." Mom wiped her forehead, leaving a splotch of grease. "Now crawl in there and turn the water back on."

"Got it." I twisted the knob.

"Okay, that's one thing checked off the list," Mom said. "If we spackle and sand today, we can paint next weekend. What color do you want for your room?"

Before I could answer, there was a loud clanging sound. "Is that the doorbell?" I asked. "It sounds like someone dropping a pan."

"Add 'new doorbell' to the to-do list." Mom headed downstairs. I followed and saw Logan through the glass panel beside the door.

The Boy Next Door is here! I shrieked inside my own head. I raced back upstairs to put my cute bomber jacket back on.

By the time I returned, Mom was sitting in the living room with Logan and his mom, who had wire-rimmed glasses and a friendly smile like her son's. "We brought cookies," Mrs. Reed said. "Welcome to the neighborhood, Natalie."

It seemed weird to call a few houses in the middle of nowhere a "neighborhood," but I didn't say so. "Thanks," I said. "You can call me Nat."

Mrs. Reed smiled at me, then turned to ask Mom about her new job. I grabbed a cookie.

"So who's that horse you were riding earlier?" I

asked Logan. "How many horses do you have?"

"Just two," Logan said. "That was Belle. Want to come meet her?"

Obviously I didn't care about meeting another big, smelly horse. But I *did* care about hanging out with the Boy Next Door.

"Sure!" I glanced at Mom. "Logan wants me to go see his horses. Is that okay?"

"Go ahead." Mom winked at Mrs. Reed. "She gets her love of animals from me. I grew up on a farm, and the neighbors had this adorable but totally obnoxious pony . . ."

I yanked Logan toward the door. "Hurry," I warned him. "Once she gets going on her childhood tales, there's no stopping her."

We walked over to his barn. Inside were two stalls, with one horse in each. Belle was a shiny, reddish-brown color with a black mane, tail, and legs, which Logan told me was called "bay" for some reason. He'd had her for years, and the two of them went trail riding a lot but also entered local shows, which was why he'd been practicing his jumping.

"So what do you do with Ghost?" I asked, lifting my hand so he could snuffle me again with his soft nose. "He's so pretty—pure white!"

"His color is called gray, not white," Logan corrected. "He's my project. I always have a second horse here—most horses, including Belle, don't like being alone."

I could relate. "What do you mean, 'your project'?" I asked.

"I take in horses who need retraining or just a little extra care and sell them when they're ready," Logan said. "That helps with Belle's expenses and my show entries and stuff."

"So Ghost needs retraining?"

"Yeah, he's a rescue. I found him at an auction, all skinny, beat-up, and lame. But now he's gained weight and is doing really well." Logan shot me a thoughtful look as I rubbed Ghost's long nose. "Come to think of it, I could use your help with something if you have time . . ."

"Sure," I said immediately. "I don't know anything about horses, though."

"Perfect." He grinned, and I wondered if it was possible he was flirting with me. What did flirting look like, anyway? I'd heard Johari's sister talk about it, but I still wasn't sure. I made a mental note to text my friends for more information.

In the meantime, I stood back as Logan led Ghost out of his stall. Then I followed them outside.

Logan led the horse into the front paddock, but I hesitated at the gate. Was I supposed to go in there with them?

At that moment, Mom and Mrs. Reed came out of our house. Mom paused when she spotted me.

"I couldn't find the teapot, so we're going over to the Reeds' house," she called.

"Hey, Ms. Morris," Logan called out politely. "Is it okay if Nat helps me with my horse?"

Mom looked thrilled. "Of course!" she replied. "Have fun, Nat!"

As she and Logan's mom disappeared into the Reeds' house, I took a careful step into the paddock. There was a pile of manure near the gate, and I wrinkled my nose as the smell wafted upward.

"What do you want me to do?" I asked Logan.

"Ghost has been doing great with me," Logan said. "I want to see how he is with other people. And he seems to like you. Would you try grooming him?"

"You mean brush him?" I stared at Ghost uncertainly. I felt sorry for him now that I knew he'd had a rough past. But this was as close as I'd ever been to such a large animal. What if he suddenly decided to trample me or something?

Logan grabbed a bucket that was hanging on the fence nearby. "Start with this," he said, shoving a brush into my hand. "Just run it over him."

I stared at the brush. Then I shrugged. Why not? If I could unclog a drain or replace a set of hinges, I should be able to clean off a horse.

"Like this?" I touched Ghost's shoulder with the brush. He flinched, and I jumped back. "Oops. Did I hurt him?"

Logan laughed. "No, you just surprised him. Here, do it like this . . ."

He put his hand over mine. I shivered, wondering if *this* was flirting. It certainly felt like it . . .

After showing me what to do, he stepped back to let me try it on my own. I did my best, brushing dust and loose hairs off Ghost's white—no, *gray*—coat.

"He likes it when I rub the brush up under his mane," I said, noticing Ghost sort of leaning into the brush. "He must be itchy there."

"Right!" Logan sounded impressed. "See? You're a natural."

I wasn't sure about that. But it felt good to hear. I only wished I didn't have to spend the whole summer at camp instead of here hanging out with Logan.

That gave me a genius idea. "I have day camp tomorrow," I told him. "But maybe I could stop by afterward to, uh . . ." Suddenly realizing I probably shouldn't say I wanted to come flirt with him, I searched for a good excuse. "Um, to sketch the horses," I blurted out at last.

"Sketch them?" Logan looked interested. "You're an artist?"

"Uh-huh. Graphic novels, mostly . . ." I went on to tell him all about Urbanna Urban.

"Cool," he said when I finished. "I usually mess around with at least one of the horses in the afternoon. And my dad works from home, so your mom probably won't mind if you hang out here, right? Let's put Ghost away and go ask her right now."

I smiled, giving Ghost one last rub with the brush. "Sounds like a plan."

Chapter 4
First Day of Camp

Mom wanted to get to work early on her first day, so she dropped me off at camp at the crack of dawn. I was the only one there except for a trio of little kids sucking on juice boxes.

"No worries, hon, let's get you all signed in and ready to go," said Madge, the head counselor, when I apologized for being early.

The day camp was located in Daisy Dell Park, which was behind the post office and consisted of a couple of tennis courts and a tetherball pole, along with some picnic tables and wooden pavilions. The rest was just fields and trees, like pretty much everything else around here. I wasn't sure why a town that was basically a park with a few buildings here and there needed an actual, official park, too, but nobody asked for my opinion.

Soon I was fully equipped with a name tag (which I stuck into my shorts pocket as soon as Madge turned away) and a schedule. "The others should start trickling in soon," Madge told me cheerfully. "Make yourself at home while you wait."

I sat down on a picnic bench and shrugged off my backpack. It took about five seconds to scan the schedule (basically, a rotating roster of arts and crafts, sports, and nature walks). There was still no sign of anyone my age arriving, so I pulled out *The Boy Next Door* to read while I waited.

But I'd only read a few panels when I got distracted by staring at a drawing of Boy. He looked sooo much like Logan, it was almost spooky.

Logan's nose is a little different, though, I realized as I studied the drawing more closely. *And Boy's ears don't stick out quite as much, and his hair is fluffier . . .*

That made me want to sketch Logan to figure out all the tiny differences. I pulled out a sketch pad and a charcoal pencil and went to work. At first, I was planning to draw Logan standing with his hands on his hips like Boy often does, but that didn't feel right. Instead, I decided to draw him riding Ghost.

It turned out to be trickier than I expected to draw a horse, even one I'd been up close and personal with. The neck didn't look right, and I couldn't quite remember which way all his legs were supposed to bend.

I was so engrossed in what I was doing that I

almost dropped my pencil when someone said, right in my ear, "Wow, that's good!"

I looked up to find a girl my age staring at my sketch. For a second I was annoyed. I wasn't shy or anything, but it seemed kind of rude to creep up on someone and peek at their drawings.

But then the girl gasped and pointed at the graphic novel lying on the bench. "Oh my gosh, *The Boy Next Door*!" she exclaimed. "That's my absolute favorite!"

"Really?" I forgot about being annoyed. "Mine too! I'm Natalie Morris, by the way. Everyone calls me Nat."

"Harper Hill." The girl pointed at herself, suddenly looking bashful. "Um, sorry to sneak up on you. But your drawing is great—except the horse's hind leg should be like this . . ." She used her finger to show me the way it was supposed to bend.

"Thanks." I quickly corrected the sketch. "Better?"

"Perfect." Harper beamed at me. She had strawberry-blond hair and wide blue eyes. "So are you new?"

"Yeah. My mom and I just moved here from Philly."

Harper's eyes got even wider. "You used to live in Philadelphia? What's that like?"

"It was great." Memories flashed through my mind, already sort of sepia-tinged and sad like an old postcard. "But I can tell you about it later. First, tell me about Daisy Dell. Do you like living here?"

"Sure." Harper shrugged. "I mean, it's okay. Just a regular place." She peered at my sketch again. "Hey, the rider you're drawing looks like Boy."

"It's not." I grinned. "It's his identical twin, also known as my new next-door neighbor, Logan Reed."

Harper gasped. "I know Logan! I mean, he's two years ahead of me in school, but everybody knows everybody around here." She leaned closer to study my drawing. "I never noticed before, but you're right—he looks exactly like Boy! Is that one of his horses?"

I nodded and touched the pencil strokes, remembering how soft the horse's nose had been and hoping I'd captured it well enough. "His name's Ghost," I said. "I don't know that much about horses, but Logan says he thinks Ghost likes me."

Harper smiled. "I have horses, too," she said softly, looking sort of shy again. "I mean, my mom and I do. My stepdad doesn't ride."

"Bragging again, Harper?" a loud voice broke in.

I looked up. Two girls our age had appeared without me noticing. One was smirking at Harper, while the other stared at me curiously.

"Who are you?" the second girl asked, tossing her long, straight black hair over her shoulder.

"This is Natalie," Harper said tentatively. "She just moved here, and—"

"Okay, thanks," the first girl said, cutting her off. She had wavy brown hair and a tiny nose. "Madge needs the new girl for something very important."

Her friend nodded. "Immediately."

"Really?" I wondered if the head counselor wanted to reprimand me for not wearing my name tag. "Uh, okay. See you later, Harper."

I grabbed my bag and followed the two girls. But we were nowhere near Madge's pavilion when they stopped.

"Whew, that was close!" the black-haired girl said.

The other nodded. "If anyone saw you with Horrid Harper, your reputation would be totally nerfed. By the way, I'm Emma Jansing, and this is Emily Patel."

"You can call us Em-and-Em," Emily said with a giggle. "Everybody does."

I frowned, catching on to what was happening. "So Madge doesn't really need to see me?"

"No, silly!" Emma smirked. "We just said that to rescue you from Horrid."

"Well, I didn't need rescuing." I hoisted my bag higher on my shoulder and glared at them. "I'd much rather hang out with Harper than a couple of mean girls—no matter what happens to my stupid reputation."

I guess most people didn't say stuff like that to Em&Em, because for a second, they just stood there with their mouths open. That was all the time I needed to spin on my heel and stomp off to find Harper.

Chapter 5
Bath Time

"...and after we finished making macramé stars, we played kickball for the last hour," I said. "Basically, it was a decent first day of camp."

"Cool." Logan glanced down from Ghost's saddle as they trotted past. I'd headed straight to his place after camp. (There was an afternoon bus for kids whose parents worked.) For the past half hour, I'd been telling him about my day while sitting on the blue barrel jump, with my sketch pad on my lap.

I'd started drawing Logan, eager to figure out the little details I'd noticed earlier. Then I remembered I'd claimed I wanted to sketch the horses. What if he asked to see? So I flipped to a clean page, figuring I'd draw Ghost first and then add Logan riding him later.

As Logan rode Ghost in a circle, I watched carefully, noting how all four legs worked together. After a few false starts, I started to get it.

Next I turned my attention—and my pencil—to Ghost's head. Before I would have said every horse looked pretty much the same, face-wise. But now I noticed that one of Ghost's nostrils was a little bigger than the other, and the hair that stuck down over his face (when I asked, Logan said it was called a forelock) curled a little bit at the ends.

I was redoing one of the horse's ears when Logan jumped down from the saddle. He walked over, leading Ghost by the reins.

"You look really focused," he said. "Can I see?"

"Sure." I held up the sketch pad. "What do you think? Does it look like Ghost?"

"Definitely!" Logan seemed impressed. "You're super talented, Nat. I can't even draw a stick figure!"

I was so busy memorizing his compliment to tell my friends later that I sort of spaced out on what he said next.

Luckily, he was still talking, and I quickly figured out the gist. He wanted me to help him give Ghost a bath.

"A bath?" I blurted out. "Like in a tub?"

Logan laughed so hard he almost dropped the reins. "No, with a hose," he said. "Want to help? You'll need to run home and put on some real shoes, though."

I glanced down at my cute, sparkly flip-flops.

"These are real shoes."

He shook his head. "Not when you're handling horses. Do you have boots? If not, sneakers will do. It needs to be something that covers your whole foot—no sandals."

It was a typical Pennsylvania summer afternoon—incredibly hot and disgustingly humid. In other words, definitely sandal weather. But I figured Logan was the horse expert, and I didn't want him to change his mind about me hanging around.

By the time I returned wearing high-tops, Ghost's saddle was off, and he was tied to the fence. Logan was hooking up a hose to a hydrant near the barn.

"Ready?" he asked, untying the horse. "This could be interesting. It's the first time I've tried this with Ghost."

"You've never given him a bath before?" I

wrinkled my nose. "No wonder he's kind of smelly."

Logan laughed as if I'd told a joke. "You can hold him while I squirt him with the hose, since he seems to like you."

"You keep saying that," I said. "But, I mean, how do you know what a horse thinks about someone?"

"Body language, mostly." He went on for a while, talking about all the details of that. I guess. To be honest, I was kind of distracted by the cute way Ghost was stretching his head toward a bucket sitting near the gate. He actually had a lot of personality— you know, for an animal.

Finally, Logan noticed, too. He picked up the bucket, which turned out to be full of carrot chunks.

"You can feed him these to keep him happy in case he doesn't like the hose," he explained. "Have you ever fed a treat to a horse before?"

When I shook my head, he showed me how to

hold my hand flat with the carrot chunk sitting on it.

"What if he eats my hand, too?" I asked, glancing from my hand—the one that I used to draw, not to mention dress and feed myself—to Ghost's mouth, full of giant teeth.

"He won't," Logan assured me. "Not if you keep it flat."

He pulled a carrot out of the bucket and showed me. Ghost carefully lifted the treat off his hand and crunched it.

So I gave it a try. The first time, I chickened out and yanked my hand away. The carrot chunk fell, and Ghost ate it off the ground.

"Sorry," I said. "Can I try again?"

This time I kept my hand steady. Ghost's lips barely grazed my skin as he took the carrot.

Something else touched my skin, though. "Ew, gross," I said, rubbing my hand on my shorts. "He totally drooled all over my hand!"

Logan just grinned. "Ready for bath time?"

I grabbed another carrot with one hand and the lead rope with the other. Ghost nudged at me, wanting the treat. I fed it to him and reached for another.

At that moment, Logan turned on the water and squirted Ghost on the shoulder. The horse was so busy looking for more carrots that I guess he didn't see it coming, because he jumped in place and let out a snort. I squeaked and skittered back out of the way, dropping the lead rope.

"It's okay." Logan grabbed the rope just in time to stop Ghost from sticking his head in the carrot bucket. "You have to hold on to him, though."

"Sorry." I took the rope—and a deep breath. "Let's try it again."

The rest of the bath went fine. Ghost didn't mind

the water, especially since I kept feeding him carrots.

"Can I try?" I asked after a while. "With the hose, I mean."

"Sure." Logan turned off the nozzle and handed it over, then took the lead rope. "Don't spray his head. Keep it low at first and work your way up."

"Okay. Like this?" I squirted Ghost's lower legs, then moved the hose up to his shoulder, then his back, and then—

"Oops!" I blurted out as the water hit Logan, who was standing behind Ghost, full in the face. "Sorry." I couldn't help giggling at his look of surprise.

"Very funny," he exclaimed. He darted around Ghost and grabbed the hose, turning it on me.

"Stop!" I half shrieked, half laughed, trying to dodge the water. My foot hit the bucket of carrots, spilling little orange chunks everywhere.

Ghost pulled away from Logan, diving toward

the spill. Meanwhile, I grabbed the hose and yanked, which made Logan lose his grip on the nozzle. It bounced off the grass, spraying both of us—and Ghost, too, not that he seemed to notice as he gobbled up every last bit of carrot. By then I was laughing so hard, I could hardly breathe, let alone try to avoid the spray.

"Okay, truce!" Logan cried at last. He was laughing, too. He grabbed the nozzle and switched it off.

"Fine." I flopped onto the grass, panting and wet and glad I'd left my sketch pad safely outside the paddock. I grinned up at Logan. He was still awfully cute in that Boy Next Door way, but he suddenly felt like an actual friend, too.

At dinner, Mom and I traded first-day stories. She seemed happy but tired and was thrilled to hear that I was hanging out with Ghost. After we loaded the dishwasher, I headed upstairs to check my texts. I'd sent Johari and Blue a couple of photos of Logan and told them about our water fight.

There was only one response, from Blue:

Cute, cute boi! Hot there, too, huh? J and I met some kids who had a fire hydrant open to cool off. She sez hi, btw, she's out shopping with her sis. L8r!

I sighed, remembering fun fire-hydrant moments we'd had over the years. Did my friends miss me as much as I missed them?

I wandered over to the window just in time to see Logan release both horses into the big field behind the barn. Ghost's clean white (gray!) coat gleamed in the light of the setting sun.

Belle started eating grass immediately. But Ghost pawed at the bare dirt by the gate, kicking up clouds of dust. He circled like a dog and then lowered himself to the ground, grunting and kicking his legs as he rolled around. When he got up and shook himself (also kind of like a dog, actually), his formerly clean coat was blotched and grimy.

I laughed. "So much for that bath," I said aloud, then grabbed my sketch pad, eager to capture the contented look on the horse's dirty face.

Chapter 6
The Flirt List

At camp the next day, our craft project was building birdhouses. I finished mine quickly—it was the kind of basic carpentry I'd been doing with Mom since I was in diapers. Harper and I were sitting with some kids she knew from school. They were nerdy and nice, and I was having fun helping them with their birdhouses.

Em&Em were at a different table. A few times, I caught them smirking in our direction, but I just focused on the task and ignored them.

"Tell me about your horses," I said to Harper as I helped a kid named Caleb straighten out the roof of his birdhouse. "What are they like? How long have you had them?"

They were the type of questions I would have asked anyone, just trying to get to know them better. But now I was more interested than before, because thinking about Harper's horses made me think about Ghost and Logan.

"My pony's name is Acorn, and he's half Shetland . . . ," Harper began. She could be kind of quiet (at least compared to me), but when she was talking about horses, she sort of lit up, like she'd be happy to talk all day.

She described Acorn and her mother's horse, Quincy. Caleb and the other kids listened for a while, but then they started arguing about some sci-fi movie they'd all seen.

"Maybe you can come over and meet Acorn sometime," Harper said to me. Then, suddenly shy again, she added, "If you want to."

"For sure!" I said. "Let's trade numbers so we can set it up." I pulled out my phone.

Harper bit her lip. "Um, I don't have a phone." Her voice was so quiet now, I could barely hear it. "I'm not allowed until I'm twelve." She shot me a sidelong look as if expecting me to make fun of her.

"No biggie." I put my phone away. "My mom can call yours. Your mom has a phone, right? We won't have to use carrier pigeons?" I grinned to show her I was kidding.

"Yeah, she does." She laughed, then picked up her birdhouse. "Hey, can you help me with the perch? I can't get it straight . . ."

At lunchtime, Harper and I flopped down on

a shady patch of grass near the water fountain. I pulled out *The Boy Next Door*, and we read it together, calling out our favorite scenes. It was fun—almost as much fun as hanging out with my old friends.

After a while, Harper crumpled her lunch bag and stood up. "Be right back. I'm going to the bathroom."

"Okay." As she hurried off, I flipped a page in the graphic novel, tracing Boy's chin with my finger. Was it maybe a little sharper than Logan's?

"Hi." A voice startled me out of my thoughts.

Squinting up against the bright midday sun, I saw Em&Em looking down at me. "Hi," I greeted them warily. What did they want?

"How's it going, Nat?" Emma asked sweetly. "Are you enjoying camp so far?"

"We heard you live next door to Logan Reed," Emily added before I could respond. "Lucky!"

Emma nodded. "He's awfully cute, don't you think?"

I shrugged, trying to play it cool. But I couldn't help smiling and glancing at the picture of Boy I'd been studying. Harper was great, but the few times I'd mentioned Logan, she hadn't seemed that interested in talking about anything except his horses. That was cool—not everyone our age was into boys yet. I mean, I barely was myself. The only boy I'd ever really noticed was Logan. And now it seemed Em&Em had noticed him, too.

"Logan's nice," I said carefully, wondering if I'd misjudged them. Maybe they weren't as mean as I'd thought. "We've been hanging out."

Emily gasped. "You have? Does he like you back?"

Whoa! Had I admitted to liking him without realizing it?

"We're friends." I climbed to my feet so I could look them in the eye without squinting into the sun. "I mean, we only met, like, three days ago."

"If you ever want to be more than friends, we can help," Emily said eagerly.

Emma nodded. "Em has two older sisters, and I've been reading my mom's *Cosmo* magazines since kindergarten," she said. "We know all the tricks."

I couldn't help being intrigued. "You mean, like . . . flirting?"

"Exactly," Emily said. "If you want Logan to notice you, you have to flirt with him. Like, you could make eye contact a lot . . ."

"And make sure you laugh at everything he says," Emma added. "Maybe talk about how many boys you knew back in Philadelphia—hey, you should be writing this down. Get out your phone."

I started a list of flirting tips in the Notes app.

I was still typing when Madge blew her whistle to start our daily nature walk.

"Good luck, Nat." Emma squeezed my arm. "Let us know how it goes, okay?"

Emily giggled. "We're rooting for you, girl."

After they left, I scanned the flirt list. Some tips seemed pretty good, like asking Logan questions about himself. Others, like falling down on purpose so he'd have to help me up, sounded kind of silly.

Em&Em seem to know what they're talking about, I thought, tucking the phone back into my pocket as I spotted Harper returning. *Still, maybe I'd better ask Johari to run these tips past her sister—just in case.*

Chapter 7
A Walk Through the Woods

As the camp bus trundled out of the parking lot, I checked my phone for the zillionth time. No new messages, even though I'd texted my friends about Em&Em's flirting tips over two hours earlier.

I pulled out my sketch pad. I'd started drawing Belle jumping, but somehow she'd turned into Ghost, so I decided to go with it. To make the picture more interesting, I drew a line of flames for him to jump over. Then I started sketching humongous wings on his back, like Pegasus.

Eight-year-old fraternal twins named Mandy and Andy were sitting across from me. "What are you drawing?" Mandy asked.

I showed her the sketch. "It's this horse I know. I might turn him into a superhero and draw him some adventures."

The idea hadn't really occurred to me until I said it, but I liked the sound of it. *The Adventures of SuperGhost*—it could be fun! Maybe SuperGhost could even meet up with Urbanna Urban sometime.

I went back to work. I was so absorbed, I almost missed the muffled buzz of a text alert. It was from Johari:

Sorry, just saw yr message. Will ask my sis asap. On my way to meet B bc big news! Mr. K wants us to help with decoration committee 4 block party!

My heart sort of twisted. Our neighborhood's

annual summer block party was totally a big deal. Somehow it hadn't occurred to me that I was going to miss it for the first time in my life. I wondered if I could convince Mom to go. It wasn't *that* long of a drive . . .

"Nat!" Mandy leaned across the aisle and poked me. "Your stop!"

"Oops." I grabbed my stuff as the bus driver peered at me in the rearview mirror. "Sorry, I'm coming!"

We'd made s'mores that afternoon at camp, so I didn't bother stopping at home for a snack before heading to Logan's. Ghost was grazing in the middle of the front paddock, while Logan rode Belle around him in a big circle. Ghost pricked his ears when he saw me, and Logan waved.

"Good, you're here," he said, before I could decide whether to try any of Em&Em's flirting tips.

"I need your help. I want to get Ghost more experience outside the ring."

"Yeah?" I was a little distracted by the cute look on Ghost's face as he walked over to me. How could I ever have thought all horses looked alike? I fed him an apple slice I'd saved from my lunch.

"I've taken him for short rides in the woods." Logan gestured toward the trees behind our houses. "He's been super sensible so far, but Belle hates when I leave her alone for too long. And I want to be able to tell people that Ghost is solid on trails. He's a little too old and plain looking to be a show horse, but I think someone would love him as a trail horse."

"Plain looking?" I exclaimed, insulted on Ghost's behalf. "Are you kidding? He's beautiful!"

"Okay." Logan shrugged. "So I was thinking we could hand-walk both horses on the trails. You leading Ghost, me leading Belle. What do you say?"

I liked the idea of a walk in the woods with Logan. Well, sort of. I'd never been anywhere wilder than Fairmount Park in Philly. Indoorsy, remember?

"Will there be bugs?" I asked. "Or snakes? Oh! What about bears? And mud and stuff?"

Logan grinned. "Yes on the bugs and mud," he said. "Probably not on the snakes and bears."

"*Probably* not?" I couldn't tell whether he was kidding.

"Come on, I'll show you what to do."

He gave me a quick lesson on how to lead a horse. It was pretty simple—basically, you hold onto the lead rope and don't let it get slack enough for the horse to step on it. Logan assured me that Ghost would be happy to follow Belle, so I wouldn't have to steer or anything.

It felt kind of scary when we stepped out of the

paddock. What if Ghost ran away, and I couldn't stop him? But he seemed happy to follow Belle, just as Logan had promised, and I quickly got used to walking along next to him, lead rope in hand.

As we headed past the barn, I noticed the doors were wide open. "Wait, don't you have to lock up?" I called out.

Logan looked back. "Huh?"

I pointed toward the barn. "You left the doors standing open. I did that at our apartment once, and Mom had a fit even though our neighbor noticed right away, and . . . Wait, why are you laughing?"

Belle seemed to be wondering the same thing. She'd stopped and was staring at her owner.

"Don't worry, city girl," Logan managed to choke out between guffaws. "I don't think anyone's going to sneak in and steal Ghost's latest pile of manure while we're gone." I guess I looked annoyed, because he finally stopped laughing. "Seriously, though, the barn door doesn't even *have* a lock."

"You don't lock it when the horses are in there? What if someone steals them?"

He shrugged. "What if there were a fire? A lock might stop someone from saving them if I wasn't home. Besides, someone could just steal them from the pasture if they wanted to. It's not really anything to worry about, though."

"Oh." I thought about what he'd said as we started walking again. Back in Philly, people locked everything up tight—apartments, cars, bicycles. Just one more difference between here and there.

We skirted the back pasture, walking between the fence and the cornfield next door, then finally reached the forest. It was another hot day, but it felt much cooler in the shade of the tall trees. We were surrounded by a tangle of vines and underbrush, but the dirt trail was wide and clear.

"My dad and I spend a Saturday every month or so doing trail maintenance," Logan said when I mentioned it.

"You did a good job." I realized I'd accidentally followed one of Em&Em's flirting tips by complimenting him. Maybe it was time to try more, since there was no telling when my friends would get back to me—preparing for the block party was a huge job, and they would probably be super busy.

I let go of Ghost's lead rope with one hand just long enough to pull out my phone, being as quiet as I could so Logan wouldn't notice. When I scanned the list, I realized most of the tips weren't practical for walking through the woods.

As I stared at my phone, I guess I wasn't paying enough attention to where I was going. My foot caught on a sticking-out tree root.

"Whoa!" I shouted, dropping the lead rope and windmilling my arms to try to prevent a face plant.

Logan spun around just in time to see me lose the battle.

"Are you okay?" Logan looked like he was trying not to laugh. As I nodded and climbed to my feet, he stopped trying. "Oh man, you should see your face!"

I smiled weakly, realizing I'd checked off another item on the flirt list: Make him laugh. Hey, I'd even done it twice!

Suddenly noticing Ghost's lead rope dangling loose, I grabbed it. "Whoa, Ghost," I said. "It's okay."

Logan stopped laughing and nodded. "That was actually a great test for Ghost," he said. "Some horses would have spooked, maybe run off. But he did great!"

I patted Ghost. He nuzzled me, as if checking that I was really okay. "He's a good boy," I crooned.

We started off again. Luckily, I'd held onto my phone better than the lead rope. As soon as Logan's back was turned, I checked the list again.

This time, I found something I could try. Em&Em had suggested making myself sound popular by talking about how many boys I'd known back in Philly.

I cleared my throat. "So did I ever tell you about my neighbor Enrique?" I asked, trying to sound casual. "He's a year older than me, but we hung out all the time. I also hung out sometimes with his friends Mikey and Owen. Oh, and I'm really good friends with this guy, Charles, at school . . ."

I kept going, naming every boy I could remember. When I finally paused for breath, Logan glanced back at me. "I bet you know a ton more people than I do, living in the big city," he said. "What's Philadelphia like? I've never been there."

"Never? Are you serious?" I was so surprised, I forgot I was supposed to be flirting. Daisy Dell sometimes seemed to exist in a whole different universe from Philadelphia. But it wasn't actually *that* far away. Harper had mentioned taking trips to the city with her parents, to visit museums or go shopping.

"Having horses makes it hard to get away." Logan smiled sheepishly. "Besides, I dunno. The big city seems kind of, you know, scary."

"No, it's great!" I told him. "I guess if you're not used to it, it might seem noisy and crowded compared to here." I glanced around at the trees and vines. "But it's amazing to be able to walk out your door and find anything you want—the latest comics from all over the world, vintage movie posters, art supplies, delicious Thai food, toilet paper, whatever. Then there are so many interesting people, and tons of stuff to do all the time . . ."

He kept asking questions about the city, and I kept answering. Ghost even seemed to join the conversation now and then by snorting or bobbing his head as we walked. I didn't realize how much time was passing until my phone buzzed—Mom was texting me to come home for dinner.

Fifteen minutes later, both horses were back in the paddock. "That was fun," I said. "And no bears! Woo!"

Logan laughed, which reminded me I was supposed to be flirting. Oops.

I tried to remember another item on the list. "Hey, what's your favorite color?" I asked.

Logan looked confused. "Uh, blue, I guess?"

"Dope." I grabbed my backpack and skipped off toward home. "See you tomorrow!"

Chapter 8
Looking Good!

When I arrived at camp on Wednesday, Harper wasn't there yet. I sat down in the shade and grabbed my sketch pad. Earlier that morning, I'd started working on a scene of SuperGhost battling a terrifying bear by shooting bolts of lightning from his hooves. I also had ideas for a story line involving a herd of shape-shifting cows that I couldn't wait to sketch out. I planned to snap a few cow photos on the bus ride home, so I'd be sure to get them right.

Who knew I'd find this kind of inspiration in the middle of Nowheresville?

I snapped a picture of the bear scene and texted it to my friends. Yesterday, I'd sent them the one of SuperGhost jumping over fire. Blue had texted back:

Legendary!

Johari had added a wow emoji and a heart.

I scrolled back to reread the only other text they'd sent yesterday, one from Blue about plans for the block-party decorations. A sharp pang of homesickness hit as I imagined all the fun they were having without me.

"Hey, Nat!" Harper rushed over, smiling and looking happy to see me. "Sorry I'm late!"

That made me feel a little better. I stuck my phone into my pocket. "Want to see my new sketches?" I asked. "I had this great idea yesterday . . ."

When the camp bus dropped me off, I ran inside to change clothes before Logan saw me. My outfit was already laid out—a pair of bright blue leggings, a blue-and-white graffiti-print tunic, blue sneakers (with blue sparkle socks sticking out), and a blue Philadelphia 76ers cap.

As I slid on several chunky blue-plastic bracelets, I glanced in the mirror. If blue was Logan's favorite color, he was going to love this!

He was riding Ghost in the paddock when I arrived. "Hi, there!" I called out, waving.

He glanced over and nodded, then returned his attention to Ghost, who was walking back and forth over a pole on the ground.

"Looking good, guys!" To give him a better view of my outfit, I climbed onto the lower rung of the fence, which caused an ominous cracking sound.

I jumped down, and Logan halted Ghost.

"Careful," he said. "The horses broke the rails over there a while back. Dad and I patched it, but you should probably sit on the barrels instead."

"Okay." I ducked into the paddock and skipped toward the barrels, adding a twirl halfway there to show off my tunic.

When I peeked at Logan, he was steering Ghost over the pole again and not even looking at me. Remembering what Johari's sister had said about boys and fashion, I figured maybe he needed a little hint.

"Hey," I called. "Do you like my hat?"

He squinted in my direction. "Sure," he said. "My dad and I watch basketball all the time. He likes the Celtics better than the Sixers, though. But listen, I'm going to do some bombproofing work with Ghost. Want to help?"

"Bombproofing?"

He must have guessed what I was thinking, because he laughed. "Don't worry, nothing to do with actual bombs. It's about teaching a horse to stay calm no matter what happens by introducing him to scary stuff a little at a time."

"Oh okay, that makes sense." I wondered how many new words I was going to learn by hanging around Logan and his horses. "Just tell me what to do."

I ran my pencil lightly over the page, shading SuperGhost's jaw. It was getting dark in my room, so I got up and switched on the light. Then I sat cross-legged on my bed, studying the drawing I'd been working on since dinner.

"Maybe SuperGhost needs a sidekick," I murmured, touching my pencil to the page again. I'd decided against the Pegasus wings, but now his back looked empty. I started drawing a rider that looked like Logan, but then I shook my head and erased. I didn't want to copy *The Boy Next Door*. This was my thing, and it needed to be totally original.

My pencil started moving again, almost with a will of its own. Before I knew it, I'd sketched in a girl rider. She had short, dark hair and a ski-jump nose, just like me.

I sat back and studied the image of me riding SuperGhost. *I wonder if riding is as fun as Logan makes it look*, I thought.

My phone buzzed. It was a text from Blue, saying that she loved the bear sketch and asking how things were going. A second later, a text from Johari popped up, too, just saying Ditto.

My thumbs flew over the tiny keypad as I filled them in. I explained the bombproofing thing— Logan had asked me to help by setting out different weird stuff, like a tarp on the ground and a plastic bag fluttering from a fence post. Then he rode Ghost around, convincing him to get closer and closer to each scary object.

My blue outfit was kind of warm for summer, so I eventually took off my hat and bracelets and rolled the leggings up into shorts. It looked kind of weird, but Logan didn't seem to notice.

He also didn't notice my attempts at flirting. At least not in a good way. I typed out to my friends:

Em&Em said to laugh at everything he says and keep tons of eye contact. I tried, but after a while, he looked at me like I had an extra head or something!

OoooO, **Johari texted back.** Sorry, forgot to talk to sis but will soon!

Ya, **Blue added.** Sorry u had a bad day!!

Tx, **I replied.** But actually, it was mostly good. Ghost kicked butt with the bombproofing stuff.

He's super brave! I think even L was impressed. He let me feed Ghost two whole apples at the end lol!

Too bad u can't ride him back to Philly for the block party, **Johari replied.** He could be in the pet parade!

Haha too bad, **I texted back.**

I added a couple of laughing emojis. But I was glad they couldn't see my real expression. I knew they didn't mean to make me feel left out.

But whether they meant it or not, that was how I felt.

Chapter 9
Sabotage

Call him by a cute, flirty nickname.

I stared at my phone, wondering if I should give up on flirting, because mostly it seemed super weird. It was Thursday, and I was sitting on the porch waiting for Mom to drive me to camp.

Next door, Logan stepped out of the barn pushing a wheelbarrow. I jumped to my feet, waving wildly.

"Yo, cowboy!" I shouted. "How's it going?"

He glanced over at me, looking very confused.

He didn't wave back, though I figured that was probably because both hands were busy with the wheelbarrow.

Just then Mom hurried outside, dressed in her white lab coat. "Later, cowboy!" I hollered as I followed her to the car.

At camp, Harper was waiting in our usual spot. "What's wrong?" she asked when she saw me. "You look, I don't know, worried."

"It's this whole Logan flirting thing . . ." I quickly outlined everything that had happened. "And so far, I don't think any of the tips are working," I finished with a sigh. "What do you think I should do?"

Harper shrugged. "I don't know much about boys and stuff. But it sounds like Ghost did great with his bombproofing!"

I could tell she wasn't that interested in talking about my flirting woes. Instead, we talked about how Harper had taken her pony, Acorn, to a bombproofing clinic once.

"We both learned a lot," Harper said. "If you want to come over sometime, I could show you some of the stuff we did. You could try it out on Ghost if Logan says it's okay."

"Sounds fun!" I said. "Maybe Mom will drive me over this weekend."

"Great," Harper said eagerly. Then her face fell. "Wait, sorry. My parents are having people over on Saturday, and Sunday, we're visiting my grandma."

"No bigs," I said with a shrug. "Maybe next weekend. Hey, want to see my latest sketches?" I reached for my bag. "How much do you know about cows?"

⬱

As I hopped off the bus that afternoon, my mind was spinning. At the end of camp, after Harper's stepdad picked her up, Em&Em had grabbed me, demanding to know whether Logan was my boyfriend yet. When they'd heard my answer, they looked dismayed.

"But you can't give up," Emily insisted.

"Yeah, boys are clueless," Emma added. "You have to keep trying until he realizes he loves you. Maybe you should bake him some cookies."

Emily nodded eagerly. "Boys love cookies!"

"Especially oatmeal-raisin cookies. I've never met a boy who wouldn't do *anything* for oatmeal-raisin cookies." Emma giggled, and Emily joined in. I wasn't sure why oatmeal-raisin cookies were so funny, and their ride came before I could ask.

So now here I was. Should I keep taking their advice, even though it hadn't worked so far?

What the heck, I thought, striding toward the paddock, where Logan was riding Ghost. I wasn't the type of person to give up on something I really wanted. And I already couldn't imagine not hanging out with Logan and Ghost.

"Yo, cowboy," I said. "What's up?"

Logan brought Ghost to a halt near the fence. "Why are you calling me 'cowboy' all of a sudden? I don't even ride Western."

I shrugged. "Just a nickname. Maybe instead I should call you, uh . . ." I searched my mind. "Cookie," I blurted out. "Speaking of cookies, I was thinking of asking my mom to bake a nice, big batch of oatmeal-raisin cookies soon. I could bring you some."

"Ew, don't bother!" Logan made a "yuck" face. "I hate raisins. One time at lunch, my friend tricked me into eating some, and I threw up in front of the whole school. Everyone called me 'Raisinface' for the next month."

First I laughed, because his story was funny. But my smile faded quickly as I absorbed what he'd said. The whole school knew about it? That had to include Em&Em. So why had they insisted I bake Logan oatmeal-raisin cookies?

Those rats! I thought as the truth dawned on me. *Those dirty, rotten mean girls aren't trying to help me. They're trying to sabotage me!*

Logan must have noticed my expression because he looked worried. "Sorry if that was rude. I just meant you don't need to bring me any cookies."

"It's okay." I patted Ghost over the fence. "Maybe I can bring you chocolate-chip muffins instead."

Logan shook his head. "Why do you want to bake me something? Between that and the weird nicknames, you're not acting like yourself today."

Ghost nudged at me to keep petting him. I focused on his sweet face so I wouldn't have to look at Logan. "Sorry," I said in a small voice. "I guess I'm just not very good at this."

"Good at what?"

Oops. That had sort of slipped out. But maybe it was for the best. I thought about Mrs. Orlov's favorite saying: *When in doubt, tell the truth.*

I took a deep breath. "I'm not very good at—at flirting." I finally looked up at him.

"Oh." His face fell. "Um, look, Nat, I just want to be friends, okay? I'm not really into, like, dating yet, or . . ." Seeming to run out of words, he dropped the reins and gestured vaguely with both hands. "You know."

I stared at Ghost again. He gazed back with wide, wise dark eyes, as if telling me he understood my humiliation.

"Don't be mad, okay?" Logan sounded worried. "The horses and I like having you around. Especially when you're not, you know . . ." His lips twitched like he was trying not to laugh. "Flirting."

"Hey, I already admitted I'm not good at it," I protested. I shot him a tentative smile. "But it's okay. I'm cool just being friends."

As soon as I said it, it was like a weight lifted off my shoulders. Who was I trying to fool, anyway? I wasn't ready for all that boy-girl stuff yet, either. Not even when the boy in question looked like my favorite Boy of all time.

That didn't mean I wanted to stop hanging out with Logan, though. Especially when Ghost was part of the package. As I stroked Ghost's soft nose, I realized what I liked about being here had as much to do with him as with Logan. Maybe even more.

That reminded me of the drawing I'd been working on last night. "So I was thinking," I said, before I lost my nerve. "Can you teach me to ride?"

Logan looked surprised. "This isn't some new way of flirting, is it?"

I stuck out my tongue. "Funny. I know I said I wanted to keep my feet on the ground. But after getting to know Ghost better, well . . ."

"I get it." Logan smiled and dismounted. "Hold him for a sec while I grab my mom's helmet—she won't mind if you borrow it."

"Um, you want to start now?"

"Why wait?" Logan tossed the reins to me, then jogged off toward the barn.

I stood there, staring up at Ghost, wondering if this was a mistake. I was a city girl. City girls didn't ride horses—did they? Ghost turned his head, blinking those wise eyes at me.

"I can do this," I whispered, rubbing his neck. "*We* can do it."

Soon Logan reappeared, holding a chunky

black riding helmet. After helping me put it on, he adjusted the stirrups on his saddle a little shorter.

Then he led Ghost to the mounting block. "Left foot in stirrup," he instructed. "Hold onto a chunk of mane to steady yourself—it won't hurt him. Swing your other leg up and over, and sit down softly."

It sounded pretty simple, so I gave it a try. "Whee, I did it!" I exclaimed as I settled into the saddle. "I'm riding!"

He laughed. "You're sitting on a horse," he corrected. "Riding is what comes next . . ."

After that, there wasn't time to think about flirting, or mean girls, or all the stuff happening without me back in Philly. Logan taught me how to hold the reins and how to squeeze with both legs to ask Ghost to walk. He began moving immediately, and I gasped, suddenly feeling very far off the ground. But Logan kept talking, urging me to relax and go with the motion.

I took a deep breath, like Blue's mom did when she was starting a yoga pose. *I'm up here, Ghost,* I thought, imagining myself as the girl from my new graphic novel. *I don't know what I'm doing yet, but I trust you. You can trust me, too. I promise.*

He flicked an ear back toward me. "See his ears?" Logan said. "That means he's listening to you."

For a second, I was afraid I'd spoken my thoughts out loud. But Logan didn't say anything else, so I figured maybe one of Ghost's superpowers was hearing even the stuff I didn't say.

After that, we worked on steering and halting. I rode Ghost in a circle in one direction, then the other. Finally, Logan let me try a short trot, which was bouncy but fun.

By then it was almost dinnertime, so I reluctantly jumped down. "Can we do another lesson tomorrow?" I asked.

"Sure." Logan smiled. "Ghost and I will be here."

"Thanks." I smiled back, wanting to hug him, but afraid he might think I was flirting again. So instead, I turned and wrapped my arms around the horse's neck. "Thanks to you, too, Ghost!"

Chapter 10
Horse for Sale

Saturday, I awoke to a coffee-and-bacon-scented house. When I got downstairs, Mom was loading a plate for me.

"Eat up," she said cheerfully. "And tell me all about your first week in Daisy Dell. It passed fast, didn't it?"

"I had my second riding lesson yesterday with Ghost. We did more trotting this time. It was fun." I sprinkled salt onto my eggs. "Logan says we can do another lesson this afternoon."

"That's wonderful." Mom sat down and stabbed at a piece of bacon. "But I've been meaning to tell you, my new boss invited us to a garden party at her house this afternoon. Sort of a welcome-to-the-clinic thing. Maybe you can have your ride before lunch."

"What? But I can't do it before lunch. Logan's going to the feed store with his parents this morning. Can't you go to your work party without me?"

Mom shook her head. "My colleagues want to meet my family." She took a sip of coffee. "That means you."

When we finished eating, Mom disappeared into her home office, and I turned on cartoons on TV and grabbed my sketch pad. I'd made a lot of progress on SuperGhost the past couple of days. I quickly finished shading a scene where he herded the mutant cows with his X-ray eyes, then flipped to a clean page to draw him galloping away.

A few minutes later, I got a text from Johari. It was pretty long, and at first I thought it was going to be flirting advice from her sister. Oops! I'd meant to let my friends know what had happened on Thursday, but I was so busy lettering the next few panels of my comic that I'd forgotten. My finger was already moving toward the response box when I realized her text wasn't about flirting at all.

Guess what? Someone moved into your old apartment yesterday.

My eyes widened, and I read on.

They're actually squeezing 3 people into that tiny place, lol! Parents & a girl our age. Her name is Chloe, and she's super nice. Blue and I took her to Hazem's to welcome her to the neighborhood. We told her all about u, too.

There was more about the new girl, but I only skimmed it. The bacon and eggs in my stomach started churning around like they were trying to escape.

Somehow I hadn't thought about someone new moving into my old home—or my old friendships. This made everything feel much more real, all of a sudden. Like Mom and I couldn't go home again even if we wanted to. This week in Daisy Dell wasn't a vacation or a test run. It was my life now, no backsies.

I stared at my phone, heart pounding, feeling like I was trapped in one of those panels from old Batman comics that was just a word like *KABLOOEY!* exploding in big letters. I needed to talk things out with someone. But this time that someone couldn't be either of my best friends, because they were part of what I needed to talk about.

Harper! I thought. I punched in her landline, but it rang and rang, and nobody answered.

I tossed aside my phone and hurried to Mom's office. She heard my footsteps and glanced up from her laptop.

"What is it, Nat?" she asked, sounding distracted. "I'm kind of right in the middle of something."

"Oh. Uh, never mind." I backed away, then turned and raced out of the house and over to Logan's, suddenly extra glad that he was a friend now instead of a crush.

I was halfway there when I remembered he wasn't home. I stopped between the house and barn, wondering what to do. Mom was busy, Harper and Logan weren't around, and none of the other kids I'd met so far felt enough like real friends for a situation like this.

But in that moment I remembered someone else—someone I only now realized was also becoming a trusted friend.

When I stepped into the barn, both horses looked up from their piles of hay. I patted Belle, then let myself into Ghost's stall.

"Hey, buddy," I whispered, running my hands along his neck. "I hope you don't mind, but I really need someone to talk to, and I know you're a good listener."

He nuzzled me, drooling half-chewed hay bits down my shirt. Taking that as him saying "Yes, go ahead," I proceeded to tell him everything. It started off being mostly about the new girl, but I couldn't help also telling him how weird it felt to move, how much I missed my old friends and my old life, how worried I was that I'd never fit in here where everything was so different . . .

By the time I got to the part about missing the block party, my arms were wrapped around his neck, and tears were streaming into his silky white mane. I didn't even worry that all the crying made my words sort of garbled. Ghost had already proved that I didn't have to say something out loud for him to understand it.

Finally, I was all cried out. "Thanks for listening, Ghost. I feel better," I said.

And you know what? It was true. Talking to Ghost really did feel like talking to a friend—maybe even a *best* friend. I'd been focused on the boy next door, but the one I was really falling for was the horse next door!

As I wiped my face with the back of my hand, my elbow bumped the stall door, which let out a rusty little rattle. "Hey, this latch is really loose," I said. "I wonder if Logan noticed. We wouldn't want you to escape."

I studied the loose latch. It was an easy fix.

"I just thought of the perfect way to thank you

and Logan for teaching me to ride," I told Ghost. "Be right back."

Moments later, I returned with our toolbox. I set to work removing the latch and reattaching it with new screws while Ghost and Belle looked on.

I was tightening the last screw when I heard voices. A moment later, Logan and his dad walked in, carrying big bags of feed. They spent a few minutes being impressed by the repaired stall door, and then another few minutes bringing in the rest of the feed.

After Logan's dad left, I told Logan about having to miss that day's lesson. "That's okay," he said. "You've already done so great with him. It made me realize how far he's come in his retraining. I mean, teaching a beginner city girl to ride?"

"What? You said I was a natural," I joked.

Logan grinned. "Anyway, I think he's ready to

move on to a new home and for me to find another horse to help." He stepped over to pat Ghost. "That's why first thing this morning, I listed him for sale on an online site."

Chapter 11
Garden Party

Mom's boss turned out to live less than ten minutes from us, though her house—or, rather, her *estate*, because that's totally what it was—seemed like a whole different world. A long, winding drive led between rows of trees to an enormous, three-story home with a tower in the middle. A couple of shutters were missing, and there were unpainted bits of siding here and there that had obviously been recently repaired. But it was still the grandest thing I'd seen in person, other than maybe City Hall back in Philly.

"Wow, this place is amazing," I said. I'd spent every moment since leaving Logan's place brooding over what he'd told me, but seeing the fancy estate almost made me forget for a second.

Almost. I still couldn't believe he wanted to sell Ghost. When I'd tried to talk him into waiting, he'd shrugged and said it was too late. Then Mom had stuck her head outside to yell for me to get ready for the party, and now here we were.

We parked and got out of the car. A bunch of people were wandering around exclaiming over a pretty old-fashioned gazebo (though it needed a paint job) and flower garden (though the picket fence bordering it was missing half of its slats).

"Did your boss just move here, too?" I wondered aloud as I waited for Mom to grab her purse from the backseat. "This place is cool but definitely a fixer-upper."

"Dr. Hernandez and her husband bought it a few years ago," Mom said. "She says their jobs are so busy that it's still a work in progress."

We followed the sound of music toward a swimming-pool deck at the side of the house. The pool itself was in good shape, though part of the deck was roped off due to rotten planks, and the mermaid statue at one end was missing an arm and part of her nose.

"They have even more home-improvement projects than us," I joked.

"Hush!" Mom smirked, then glanced around to make sure nobody had heard. "Look, there are some kids—why don't you go say hi?"

About a dozen kids were in or near the pool. They ranged from toddlers splashing in the shallow end to teens lounging on pool chairs. Standing to the side watching the others was . . .

"Harper!" I blurted out in surprise.

She looked up and waved. "Nat!" she exclaimed, rushing toward me. "What are you doing here? I told you my mom's having people over today."

"Yeah, you told me," I said. "So what are *you* doing here?"

She blinked, looking confused. "Um, I live here?"

I gasped, finally catching on. "Wait," I said. "Is Dr. Hernandez your mom?"

We both talked at the same time for a while as we worked out what was going on. Dr. Hernandez had changed her last name when she'd married Harper's stepdad. That was why it had taken us so long to realize Harper's mom was my mom's new boss!

Finally, Harper grabbed my hand, pulling me

away from the pool. "Since you're here, come meet Acorn!"

At the back of the house was an enormous pasture, probably five times as large as the one behind Logan's barn. A bay horse and a stout, reddish-brown pony were grazing there.

"I'll get them so you can meet them," Harper said eagerly. She led me into a huge, old-fashioned barn. Unlike Logan's little barn, where every inch of space was used for something, Harper's was mostly a vast open space. Two stalls were built into one wall, and hay was stacked against another. There was a ramshackle wooden cabinet by the stalls. The door was standing open, and I could see saddles and other horse stuff inside.

"Sorry, it's a mess—we really need to fix it up, but there are so many things to do in the house, so . . ." Harper looked embarrassed as she glanced around.

"No, it's amazing!" I spun on my heel, taking it in. "You could fit a huge herd of horses in here. Or maybe a small herd of elephants!"

"The people who lived here before us collected antique cars," Harper explained. "They took out most of the stalls so they could park in here."

She slid open a pair of tall doors that opened directly into the pasture. When she whistled, the horse and pony raised their heads, then trotted toward us.

Acorn was adorable, with a shaggy mane and bright eyes. Quincy was ridiculously tall, though Harper seemed unfazed as she shooed the big horse into one of the stalls.

She left Acorn out, and the pony seemed content to nose around for stray bits of hay on the floor while we patted him and talked. "I tried to get out of coming to this party," I admitted. "But that was before I knew you'd be here. See, I just found out something terrible . . ."

I told her about the sale ad. "Oh no!" Harper looked stricken. "But you were just learning to ride on him!"

"I know. I had another great lesson yesterday after camp." I filled her in on the details. With every word, it seemed more and more impossible that Ghost could be leaving my life so soon. It felt almost as terrible as leaving my friends back home. A week ago, I probably wouldn't have believed I could feel that way about a horse. But that was before I got to know Ghost.

"He sounds like a great horse," Harper said.

"I can't believe Logan's selling him." I rubbed Acorn's neck. "I wish I could buy him myself."

Harper laughed uncertainly. "Wait—do you mean that?"

Did I? I thought about it, but only for a second. "I guess not," I said with a sigh. "I just wish he could stay."

Harper ran her fingers through her pony's bushy forelock. "I can't even imagine what it would be like if I had to sell Acorn. Maybe you should talk to your mom about it."

I shrugged. "Mom did say I could get a pet," I said, only half joking. Maybe even less than half. "And I have some money saved up . . ."

"I can help!" Harper said eagerly. "We could figure out how to convince your mom."

I didn't answer for a second, staring at Acorn but actually picturing Ghost. Me, a horse owner? A week ago, I never could have imagined it. Even now, I was having serious trouble.

But I also couldn't imagine life without my Horse Next Door.

Chapter 12
Moneymaker

When I went over to Logan's on Sunday morning, he had both horses tied to the paddock fence. Belle was fully tacked up, and Logan was carrying Ghost's saddle out of the barn.

"Oh good, you're here," he greeted me. "I was thinking we'd go on a trail ride today."

"A trail ride? Me?" I said. "But I've only had two lessons!"

"You'll be fine." Logan hoisted the saddle onto

Ghost's back. "I want to be able to add 'trail ridden by a beginner' to the online ad."

My stomach clenched at his mention of the ad, and I almost blurted out that I wanted to buy Ghost. But I bit my tongue. Harper and I had agreed to spend the whole week figuring out a plan, and I didn't want to tell anyone else, even Logan, until we'd worked out the details.

"How soon do you think someone will buy Ghost?" I asked, trying to sound casual, as Logan buckled the girth.

"Hard to say," he said. "My last project took almost two months to sell. Sometimes it takes even longer."

Good, I thought, feeling a little less panicky. *So we have time.*

When both horses were ready, Logan helped me mount, then led Belle over and opened the gate.

He swung into the saddle. "Just stay behind me," he called over his shoulder. "Keep your heels down and sit up straight. Ghost will do the rest."

Harper and I made a great team. Monday at camp, we spent lunch break figuring out how much more money I still needed to buy Ghost. Luckily, I'd been saving up to attend a big comics convention later in the summer. The con was back in Philly, so I figured I probably couldn't go. And even if I could talk Mom into driving me back, I realized I'd rather spend my savings to buy Ghost.

"You still need more, though," Harper said as we pored over the numbers. "Not just to buy him, but you'll have pay to board him somewhere, too."

I'd already thought about that. "I'm going to ask Logan if I can board him at his barn," I said. "That way I can see him every time I look out my window.

And since I'll be paying to keep him there, Logan won't need to take in another project horse to make money. Maybe I can even convince Mom to chip in the amount she would've paid for dog food."

Harper clapped. "Genius!" she exclaimed. "I can donate my allowance, too. It's not much, but—"

"No, I can't take your money. I really appreciate it, but it wouldn't be right."

Harper looked a little hurt. "Okay."

"It's really nice of you to offer!" I grabbed her hand and squeezed it. "But I need to buy Ghost myself. I definitely still want your help figuring out how to earn more, though."

"Good." Harper gave me a tiny smile. "Because I had another idea. What if you offered to draw funny caricatures of people here at camp? You know—like the artists you see at carnivals or on the boardwalk at the shore?"

"Oh wow, now you're the genius!" I exclaimed. "That sounds a lot more fun than anything I came up with." I grabbed my sketch pad and a charcoal pencil. "Let's start right now!"

By Tuesday, the entire camp knew about my caricature business, and I think most had already had me draw them. On Wednesday, kids started bringing in orders from friends, siblings, and even parents.

"You can do it from a photo, right?" asked a kid named Jonathan, who was friends with Em&Em but seemed nice, anyway. "My dad wants to surprise my mom, and her birthday's tomorrow."

"Sure," I said. "Text me the photo, and I'll get it to you by the end of the day."

By Thursday, my drawing hand was so tired, I could hardly hold a pencil. But our business was booming, bringing us closer to our goal.

I was sketching a funny caricature of my new camp friend, Caleb, in a Star Trek pose when Harper rushed over. "Brianna Elliot wants you to draw her with her pet goat," she said breathlessly.

Even though drawing all those caricatures kept me busy, I made sure to spend time with Ghost every afternoon. For one thing, my hand needed to rest. For another, I wanted to be as good a rider as possible by the time Ghost was mine. Sure, Logan would still be right there to help. But if I was going to be a horse owner, I wanted to be a good one. I got Logan to teach me how to put on the saddle and bridle, how to feed the horses, and even how to clean stalls. And you know what? That zoo smell I'd noticed the first day didn't seem so bad anymore.

By Friday afternoon, I was feeling pretty good. My caricatures were still a hit. I was working on one for Madge, the camp counselor, when Brianna Elliot tapped me on the shoulder on her way off the bus.

"See you tomorrow, Nat," she said. "Halima and I can't wait!"

"Me too," I said with a smile. "Don't forget your sleeping bag!"

Harper and I were having a sleepover the next night to brainstorm more moneymaking ideas, and she'd also invited Brianna and her friend Halima Faez, since she said they were two of the smartest kids in our class and might have good ideas. We were planning to sleep out in Harper's big old barn with the horses. I couldn't wait!

I was thinking about which pajamas to pack for the sleepover as I entered Logan's barn a few minutes later. Belle looked up briefly, then returned to eating her hay. But Ghost left his hay pile, stepped up to the stall door, and nickered.

I smiled. "Hey, SuperGhost." I hurried over to rub his face. "I'm happy to see you, too."

Using his nickname made me realize I'd barely worked on my graphic novel all week. But it could wait. Once Ghost was mine, I'd have all the time in the world to create more adventures for us.

Just then Logan burst in, grinning from ear to ear. "Hey, Nat, guess what?" he exclaimed. "I just talked to a lady who runs a lesson barn in the next county over. She said Ghost sounds perfect for her program. She's picking him up next week!"

Chapter 13
Won't Give Up

I clung to Ghost's stall door, fearing I might fall over in shock. "What?" I said, hoping I'd heard him wrong. "She's buying him?"

"Well, taking him on trial for now." Logan stepped over to give Ghost a pat. "But she's looking for a quiet beginner-lesson horse, and he's perfect for that." He nudged me with his shoulder. "You proved that, right?"

I shook my head. "But you said it would take

121

months to sell him!"

"Sometimes it does. Sometimes you get lucky." Logan was still grinning. "Hear that, Ghost? You're going to be a lesson horse!"

"No!" I cried so loudly, it startled a bird roosting in the rafters. "You can't sell Ghost to that lady. Because *I* want to buy him!"

Logan's smile disappeared, then returned, then faded again. "You what? Come on, Nat. This is serious."

"I *am* serious," I exclaimed. "I was going to tell you, but I wanted to save up more money first."

Logan scratched his head, making his hair stand up in tufts. "But you just started riding. How could you—I mean, it's kind of—I don't even know what to say."

"Say you'll keep him a little longer," I begged, grabbing his arm. "I promise I'll have the money soon!" I told him how much I'd already saved up. He sort of grimaced, and I could guess why—it was only about half the price from the ad. Even if I agreed to borrow Harper's allowance money, it wouldn't be nearly enough.

"Sorry, Nat." Logan gently twisted his arm out of my grip. "The thing is, I already found a new project horse. My parents are taking me to see him tomorrow morning." He smiled uncertainly. "His owners lost their farm and can't afford to feed him, so he really needs me."

"But Ghost needs you, too," I said. "Or at least I need Ghost."

"Ghost will have a great home at the lesson barn. And you can help me with the new horse, okay? His name's Comet."

"I don't care what his name is. I don't want to help with some other horse." My eyes filled with tears as I gazed at the adorable gray horse leaning his head over the stall door, watching me. "I want Ghost."

Logan didn't say anything for a moment. Then he shrugged. "Ghost isn't leaving until Monday," he said. "I could give you another lesson on him today, if you want."

I hesitated, remembering how great it felt to sit on Ghost's broad back; how much fun it was to figure out how to talk to him with my legs and the reins. How I forgot about everything else while I was up there.

But then I shook my head. I couldn't ride him again and fall even more in love with him. Not when I might never see him again after this weekend.

"Thanks." My voice came out all froggy as I did my best not to burst into tears. "But I-I have to go home now."

I turned and fled.

 ∽

An hour later, I was doodling hearts into the margins of *SuperGhost* and feeling slightly less hopeless. Why was I giving up so easily? That wasn't like me. Logan's news had taken me by surprise, that was all.

Mom did say we could get a pet, I reminded myself, checking the time to see how soon she'd be home. *And she seems super psyched that I'm interested in horses. Logan hasn't even met that other horse yet. I'm sure I could change his mind . . .*

The more I thought about it, the more optimistic I felt. Mom's new job paid more than her old one, and it had to be cheaper to live way out here in Nowheresville. Maybe if I asked really nicely, she'd help me pay for Ghost.

But when Mom came home, three new friends from work were with her. There was another

PA from the practice, one of the nurses, and the receptionist—a woman who told me to call her Bunny and then never gave me the chance to call her anything because she never stopped talking.

They swept me out of the house and off to a local Italian restaurant for dinner. I sat there listening to them (well, mostly Bunny) gossip about the office, picking at my spaghetti and wondering when I'd have a chance to talk to Mom in private.

By the time we got home, it was way past my usual bedtime, and Mom was yawning and didn't even insist we tidy up downstairs before heading to bed. I decided talking to her about Ghost would have to wait until morning.

Chapter 14
Mom to the Rescue?

"Geez Louise, Mom," I muttered, checking the clock on my phone for the zillionth time. Almost nine o'clock. "Are you ever going to get up?"

Mom didn't usually sleep much past six thirty, even on weekends. But once in a while she let herself have what she called "makeup sleep," and on those days she could be in bed as late as ten or eleven.

I was tempted to wake her up. This was important! But I knew she'd be in a better mood if she got to sleep in. To distract myself, I checked for new texts. I'd texted Johari and Blue last night before bed, telling them what was going on with Ghost, but neither had answered yet.

"Oh duh," I murmured as I realized there was a good reason for that. Today was the block party!

It was weird to think about everyone back in Philly gathering together and having fun without me. I closed my eyes and could almost smell the burgers and empanadas frying and hear Blue's cousin's band warming up. It was a hot, sunny summer day in Daisy Dell. Was it the same at the block party? Would someone open the fire hydrant in front of the laundromat to cool off?

Thinking about what I was missing made me feel restless and sad. Even my sketch pad couldn't hold my attention. Finally deciding that I needed to stretch my legs and get fresh air, I let myself out of the house and wandered over to Logan's barn.

Both horses were grazing in the front paddock, but I didn't see Logan. When I remembered why, my heart sank. He was visiting that other horse. I needed to get Mom on my side before it was too late.

I pulled out my phone, planning to ask her to text me as soon as she woke up. At that moment, the phone vibrated in my hand with a text from an unknown sender. Curious, I opened it.

> Hey, Nat, this is Emma. Ems and I want u to do one of yr funny pics of us. Maybe posing with one of L's horses. Cute, amirite? So u busy right now?

I blinked at the text in surprise. Even though practically everyone else at camp was my new best friend thanks to the caricatures, I'd barely spoken to Em&Em all week. Were they trying to make up for being so awful before by hiring me for a caricature now?

I was tempted to ignore the text. But just then, Belle let out a squeal as she nipped at Ghost, who playfully kicked up his heels in response. Watching the horses play made me realize I needed every penny I could earn.

At Logan's rn, I texted back. Can meet u here but has to be soon.

The response came almost immediately.

B right there!

I texted Mom, then went to pat Ghost over the fence. "Oh, Ghost," I whispered, playing with his forelock. "I hope I can convince Mom that we have to buy you. Because I don't think I can stand losing you so soon after finding you." As I stared into his soulful dark eyes, I thought back to the first time I'd seen him through my new bedroom window. Had that really been only two weeks ago? "You're more than a horse to me," I told him, knowing he understood even if nobody else would. "You're what makes this weird new place feel a little more like home..."

I was still talking to him ten minutes later when Em&Em arrived on their bikes.

"What's up?" Emma greeted me, her eyes darting around. "So where's your *boyfriend*, Logan?"

"Nat and Logan, sittin' in a tree," Emily sang loudly.

"K-I-S-S-I-N-G!" Emma joined in, making smoochy lips for extra emphasis.

"Logan, Nat wants to marry you!" Emily shouted.

Emma giggled. "Gee, I hope Logan doesn't hear us—that would be totes embarrassing for you!" She kept looking around as if Logan might pop out of the barn or house at any second.

"Logan's not here," I spat out, realizing they'd tricked me again, which annoyed me almost as much as their behavior. "And even if he heard your silly song, he wouldn't care. He's my *actual* friend, unlike you two jerks! Don't you have anything better to do than bully the new girl?"

My voice was even louder than Emma's. Behind me, I heard a thud and a snort. Both horses were running around and bucking. All the shouting must have set them off again.

"Easy, guys!" I cried as Belle chased Ghost toward the section of fence with the creaky boards. "No, not that way—stop!"

I raced around the paddock, waving both arms like Logan had taught me to stop the horses from running into the fence. But as Ghost spun around to dodge past Belle, he kicked up his heels again, and I heard the crack of his back hooves hitting the boards—breaking through the weak spot.

Em&Em glanced at each other with a smirk,

then they started swinging their arms and whistling. At first I had no idea what they were doing.

Then my eyes widened as I realized they were trying to scare the horses through the broken fence!

When one of the girls tossed a handful of dirt into the paddock, Belle bolted wildly, bucking and snorting. She kicked out at Ghost as she passed, sending him jumping to one side. That put him right next to the hole in the fence, and before I knew it, he was stepping out over the broken boards!

Meanwhile, Belle skidded to a stop at the far end of the paddock. She spun around and whinnied at Ghost, then trotted back toward the hole in the fence. I gulped, imagining her following him out, and then the two of them galloping off into the woods, or worse yet, onto the road.

"Whoa!" I yelled, waving my hands as I raced toward the opening, only vaguely aware of Em&Em

jumping on their bikes and pedaling away, cackling.
I was totally focused on Belle. I didn't know her like
I knew Ghost. I didn't fully trust her. But if she got
out, there was no way I'd be able to catch them both.

My hands were shaking as I blocked the opening
in the fence with my body, still waving my arms. For
a second, I was afraid Belle would run right over me.

But she skidded to a stop, then turned and
ran along the fence line, whinnying at Ghost. He
whinnied back this time, prancing in place.

"What's all the commotion out here?"

It was my mom, bleary-eyed, rumple-haired,
and still in her nightgown. "Mom!" I cried. "Ghost
got out, but I can't go get him or Belle will escape,
too."

Luckily, Mom was already catching on. She took
over for me at the broken fence, talking soothingly
to Belle while I went to catch Ghost.

"Oh, Ghost," I said with a relieved sigh when he lowered his head and let me grab his halter to lead him into the barn. "Thank goodness you're okay."

It took Mom and me half an hour to repair the fence well enough to hold until Logan got new rails. She'd run home to change clothes and grab our tools while I kept an eye on the horses. While we worked, I told her everything.

"So I was hoping you'd help me buy him," I finished. I glanced toward the barn, where I could see Ghost in his stall through the open door. "Because I don't think I can stand it if he goes away forever."

Mom sighed and dropped a roll of wire back in her tool kit. "Oh, Nat," she said. "I understand how you feel. It just about killed me to leave my neighbors' pony behind when we moved away. But I just don't know . . ."

Before either of us could say anything else, the Reeds' car pulled in. Logan and his parents came over to see what was happening, and when they heard the story, Mr. and Mrs. Reed insisted on paying me for fixing the fence.

"We should have repaired it properly a year ago," Mr. Reed said ruefully. "This was bound to happen sooner or later." He winked and pressed some bills into my hand. "You can share this with your mother if you like."

My eyes widened when I saw several twenty-dollar bills. "Hey, Logan," I blurted out, doing some quick calculations in my head and adding in Harper's allowance money, which I knew she'd let me borrow. "If I can owe you, like, fifty bucks, I think I have enough to buy Ghost now."

"Really?" Logan shrugged. "I mean, if you're

serious, that's close enough. I mostly want him to have a good home."

My heart jumped. But Mom held up a hand. "Nat, wait. We haven't finished talking about this. I know I said you could get a pet, but we can't exactly build Ghost a kennel in the backyard."

"That's okay," I told her. "He can stay right here at Logan's!"

"No, he can't," Logan said. "I just told Comet's owners I'd take him. They're dropping him off on Monday. You can buy Ghost if you want, but you'll need somewhere else to board him. I only have room for two."

Chapter 15
The Sleepover

"So Mom said it was happening too fast." I pressed the phone closer to my ear, not wanting Harper to miss a word. "She said maybe I should take riding lessons for a while first. I have to convince her to change her mind!"

"I understand," Harper said. "Maybe we can figure it out tonight at the sleepover."

In all the commotion, I'd totally forgotten about the sleepover. I hesitated, trying to figure out how to tell Harper I couldn't go. If I stayed home and talked to Mom, maybe I could make her see how important Ghost was to me.

Before I could say anything, Harper continued. "You can still come early, right?" she asked. "I really want to fix the tack cabinet and that broken window before Brianna and Halima get there. They've never been to my house, and I don't want them to think it's a total dump . . ."

Her voice trailed off at the end. She sounded nervous, and for a second I couldn't figure out why.

Then I got it. Harper was shy. I was so opposite-of-shy myself that I sometimes forgot that.

She got to know Brianna and Halima better because of the caricatures, I realized. *Inviting them to a sleepover would be easy for me, but it is probably really scary for her. She wants to make a good impression, and I promised to help her.*

I couldn't ditch her now. Not after she'd done everything she could to help me. Getting the horse of my dreams wasn't worth letting down a good friend.

"Of course," I said. "I'll see you soon."

~

"Are you sure this is safe?" I carefully stepped over a fallen branch.

Mom glanced back with a smile. She was on the wooded trail a few steps ahead. "Don't be silly," she said. "I used to hike like this all the time at your age. Besides, didn't you and Logan ride the horses out here?"

"That's different." I'd been surprised when Mom had suggested walking to Harper's house instead of driving. Apparently Harper's mom had told her it was only a fifteen-minute hike if we took a shortcut through the woods. "But now that you mention horses . . ." I took a deep breath. "Can we talk about Ghost?"

She stopped, waiting for me to catch up. Her face was serious as she looked down at me. "Good idea," she said. "Nat, I wish I could help you do this. I really do. I even asked Mrs. Reed what we'd be getting ourselves into."

"Yeah?" I held my breath and crossed my fingers.

Mom shook her head sadly. "I'm sorry, baby, but it's just not practical right now. All the boarding barns we can afford are at least half an hour's drive away, and with me working full-time, you'd never get to see Ghost anyway."

"But I could go on weekends," I protested, kind of shocked that she'd even considered it. That meant there was still a chance, right? "Or maybe I could find someone to carpool with, or—"

"I'm sorry, Nat." Mom shrugged. "Logan said you

could help him with his new horse, right? Maybe if you stick with it, we can figure something out down the road."

"But Ghost will be gone by then," I exclaimed. "I don't just want *a* horse—I want *this* horse. He needs me. And I need him." I sort of didn't want to say the next part, because I didn't want to make her feel bad for moving us out here. But I needed her to understand. "Being with Ghost makes me feel like I belong here," I told her. "Like this place is actually, you know, a real home, with one real thing I can count on to be there just for me."

Mom reached out and pushed a strand of hair off my forehead. "There's really nothing like your first heartbreak, is there?" she murmured. "I'm so sorry, baby. It's just not in the cards right now."

There were tears in her eyes and definitely in mine, too. Because it was finally sinking in: It was over. This wasn't a graphic novel where a hero like Boy could solve any problem by the end of the story.

Ghost was leaving, and there was nothing I could do about it.

Harper and I spent a couple of hours repairing the tack cabinet, replacing a cracked windowpane, and sweeping away layers of dust and dirt. While we worked, I told her what Mom had said, and we talked it out a little, but there really wasn't much to say. It helped knowing she knew how I felt, though.

Just before the other girls were due to arrive, Harper's parents came out bearing sleeping bags and baskets of snacks. "Wow, you girls really gave the place a facelift," her mom said.

Harper's stepdad chuckled. "Harper told us you were handy, Nat," he said. "But this is beyond handy. You should probably drop out of school now and start your own contracting business."

"Ronnie!" Harper's mom poked him on the shoulder and laughed. "Don't let her mother hear you say that!"

Brianna and Halima arrived a few minutes later, and the party was in full swing. But I was still feeling sad, and since I didn't want to bring the others down, I said I'd had an artistic brainstorm and needed to get it down on paper before I lost it. I spent the next hour lying on my stomach on the far side of the barn, sketching an action scene of SuperGhost leaping across a river to rescue a lost calf. Even if Ghost and I couldn't be together anymore, I still wanted to finish my graphic novel. At least it would give me something to remember him by.

Footsteps creaked on the old barnwood floor. "Hey, that's really good," Brianna said, pushing her glasses up her nose.

"Thanks." I looked across the barn to where Harper and Halima were giggling together. "Oops, I said I'd help with the stalls, didn't I? Sorry."

"It's okay. We're almost done," Brianna said. "Come see!"

She led me over to the other girls. We'd decided that if we were going to sleep in the barn, we should each have a "stall," marked out on the floor by some sparkly craft tape Halima had brought.

"Looks gre-e-e-a-at!" I said, turning the word into a whinny. I stepped into one of the sparkly squares and dropped to my hands and knees, pretending to be a horse.

The others giggled and did the same. "Where's my hay?" Halima demanded, pawing with her front "hoof."

We made such a racket that Acorn lifted his head to peer at us over the wall of his (real) stall.

Brianna and Halima were chasing each other around pretending to be racehorses, and I was patting Acorn when Harper sidled over to me. "You okay?" she whispered.

I slung an arm around her shoulders. No matter what else I thought about moving to Daisy Dell, I'd never regret meeting her. Or Ghost, for that matter, despite how things had turned out.

"I'm great," I said, hugging my new friend tight. "Super great."

We stayed up telling ghost stories, eating tons of snacks, and braiding the leftover sparkly tape into wreaths for the horses' stalls. Eventually Halima started yawning so often her mouth was open more than it was closed. Then Brianna snuggled into her sleeping bag, "just to rest my eyes," and was snoring seconds later.

"I guess we should go to sleep," Harper said. "Good night, guys."

"Good night," I murmured, sliding my legs into my own sleeping bag.

The only responses were soft snores and mumbles. I smiled as I glanced down the line of "stalls." My eyes were drifting shut when I felt my phone vibrate under my pillow. I pulled it out and was surprised to see a text from Johari.

Sorry so late, it said.

A second later, another text appeared, this one from Blue. Just back from block party. Super fun!

I rolled my eyes. It was bad enough I was losing Ghost; I wasn't in the mood to be reminded how much I was missing back home. But Johari's next text made me forget about that:

We couldn't wait until tmw to tell u the big news! B and I set up a hair-braiding booth, and we made tons of $$$. It's for you—we want to help u buy your big, smelly horse!

A second later, Blue chimed in again with the exact amount they'd raised. When I saw the number, my eyes widened in shock.

"Are you still awake?" Harper whispered. "I can see your phone light."

"Sorry," I whispered back, wiggling my sleeping bag over to her. "But you'll never guess what my amazing friends did for me!"

I showed her the texts, quietly explaining about the block party. "Wow!" Harper whispered. "That's definitely enough to cover a couple months' board."

I nodded, hardly believing Johari and Blue had done this. They were such amazing friends—why had I ever thought a little distance could change that?

But my elation wore off quickly as I realized there was still one serious problem. I told Harper what my mom had said about the lack of affordable boarding barns nearby. "The places she found were way too far to ride my bike. And with no space for a third horse at Logan's . . ."

I guess we weren't being as quiet as I thought, because Brianna sat up and yawned. "Hey," she said, pointing at me. "You're out of your stall. Naughty pony." Then she flopped back down and started snoring again.

Her words jolted something loose in my mind. I glanced down the line of fake stalls, then stared at Harper. She stared back at me.

"Are you thinking what I'm thinking?" I whispered.

"I think maybe I am," she whispered back. "And it's perfect!"

Chapter 16
He's All Mine

The following Friday afternoon, I gave one last tap with my hammer and stepped back. "What do you think?" I called.

Harper hurried over to see my handiwork. I'd just hung a hand-lettered wooden sign on the front of one of the three stalls in the Reeds' huge, old barn.

Yes, I said *three* stalls. The sparkle-tape stalls from the sleepover had made us realize that while Logan's barn was too small for three horses, Harper's had plenty of room. I had more than enough building skills to create another stall right beside Acorn's. And that was exactly what I'd done, with Harper, her dad, and my mom helping out.

And now that third stall belonged to Ghost!

It had all happened so fast—Harper had run inside to talk to her parents first thing Sunday morning after the sleepover. Her mom had immediately called my mom, who had called Logan's mom. Within an hour, it was all settled. Logan would sell Ghost to me, and I would board him at Harper's!

And now here was Ghost—*my* Ghost—nibbling hay in his new stall. I stared at him, still not quite believing it could be true. But the sign I'd just hung, which spelled out his name and mine, proved it.

"The sign looks perfect." Harper checked her watch. "And you finished just in time. Bri and

Halima will be here soon."

"Logan, too." I dropped the hammer in my tool bag. "Let's get tacked up!"

Mom had bought me my very own beautiful, brand-new pink-and-white-checked saddle pad and matching pink riding helmet to celebrate buying Ghost, though I was still borrowing a saddle from Harper and a bridle from Logan until I could save up for my own. All my money had gone to Ghost's purchase price, and I'd need the money my Philly friends had raised to pay for hay, grain, and bedding (though Mom was chipping in, too). Luckily, Harper's parents weren't charging me anything to stay at their barn except an hour or two of work around the estate each weekend. With Harper and her stepdad helping, I'd already fixed the flower-garden fence and started work on the pool deck. There was so much more to do that I figured I'd be able to work off Ghost's board forever!

I was a little sad that I couldn't look out my bedroom window and see my horse next door anymore. But in a way this was even better, because now Harper and I could ride together. The trails I hiked to get to Ghost's new home were already almost as familiar as the streets and alleys back in Philly.

As I lifted the bridle toward Ghost's head, he flapped his lips and made a funny face. I laughed, slung the bridle over the edge of the stall, and reached for my sketch pad to capture his expression. It would be the perfect look for the moment when SuperGhost faces off against a flock of ghostly squirrels!

As I was sketching, there was a clatter of hooves outside, followed by several voices. Then Brianna hurried into the barn.

"Halima, Logan, and I are here," she said. "You guys ready?"

"Just about," I replied, tossing aside my sketch pad and grabbing the bridle. "Okay, Ghost. I hope I can get all these straps and buckles right this time . . ."

I was getting good at putting on the saddle, but the bridle was trickier. Harper led Acorn out of his stall and came over to watch.

"Perfect," she said as I slid the last strap into its keeper. "Do you need me to double-check your girth?"

"No thanks, I think it's tight enough." I slid my hand between the padded leather girth and Ghost's belly to make sure, just as Logan and Harper had taught me. Then I followed my friend as she led her pony out into the sunshine.

Logan was sitting in the saddle of his new project

horse, Comet, who was an adorable black-and-white pinto. When Halima and Brianna had heard the three of us were planning a trail ride, they'd asked to hike along just for fun.

"We're ready," I called to my friends. "I just need to pull my stirrups down."

"No hurry." Logan grinned and patted his back pocket. "I brought along some reading material in case we had to wait."

I grinned back as I recognized the graphic novel sticking out of his back pocket. It was *The Boy Next Door*! I'd finally remembered to tell Logan how much he reminded me of the main character, and he'd been curious enough to borrow my copy.

"Need help mounting?" Harper asked as she watched me pull down the stirrups.

I shook my head. "I'm okay," I said. "Ghost always stands still while I get on. Right, buddy?"

Ghost turned his head at the sound of his name. I gazed into his dark, wise eyes, suddenly almost breathless knowing that now he was all mine. *How did I get so lucky?* I wondered. I slung the reins over his head, using that as an excuse to give him a quick hug.

Once Harper and I had mounted, the five of us crossed the lawn and headed into the woods where it was shady and cooler.

"It's so gorgeous out here," Halima commented, bending to pluck a wildflower, which she tucked behind her ear. "What a perfect place to hike."

I glanced around, taking in the peaceful, tall trees and a bird fluttering in the underbrush. "I can't believe I used to think the woods were scary," I said.

"You did?" Brianna sounded surprised. "What's scary about a bunch of trees?"

"Nothing, but I didn't know that, since I'd never

really spent any time in the country until we moved here," I said. "All I knew was being a city girl."

Halima hopped over a root. "Do you miss living in the big city?"

I thought for a second before answering. "I definitely still miss it, especially my friends." I smiled, recalling my latest texts with Johari and Blue. They were almost as excited about me buying Ghost as I was, and they were planning a road trip out to visit me before school started. "And I miss my favorite restaurants and comic-book shop and how busy and exciting things are." I leaned forward to rub Ghost on the neck, and one ear quirked back toward me in response. He was always listening! "But this place is amazing in a whole new kind of way."

I looked at Daisy Dell differently now that I was starting to feel at home here. Did that mean I was seeing myself differently, too?

I'm absolutely still an artist, I thought. *And a nerd. But maybe I'm only half city girl now, and the other half is becoming a country girl.* I ducked to avoid a low-hanging branch and waved away the spiderweb dangling from it. *I'm definitely not quite so indoorsy anymore!*

"We're coming to a clearing," Harper called from the front of the line. "Should we do a little trot?"

"Definitely!" I called back, shortening my reins and getting ready for the faster gait, grinning at Logan as he glanced back to check on me.

That reminded me of one other way I'd for sure changed since moving here. Whatever else I might be, Daisy Dell—and the boy next door, and my new friend Harper, and, most of all, my very own SuperGhost—had turned me into a hardcore horse girl!